To my mom, my dad, and my husband, Brice.

Copyright © 2019 Anne Lambelet

First published in 2019 by Page Street Kids,
an imprint of
Page Street Publishing Co.
27 Congress Street, Suite 105
Salem, MA 01970
www.pagestreetpublishing.com

Distributed by Macmillan, sales in Canada by The Canadian Manda Group

19 20 21 22 23 CCO 5 4 3 2 1

ISBN-13: 978-1-62414-656-5
ISBN-10: 1-624-14656-2

CIP data for this book is available from the Library of Congress.

This book was typeset in Kefa.
The illustrations were done in pencil and digital media.

Printed and bound in Shenzhen, Guangdong, China

Page Street Publishing uses only materials from suppliers who are committed to
responsible and sustainable forest management.

Page Street Publishing protects our planet by donating to
nonprofits like The Trustees, which focuses on
local land conservation.

Maria the Matador

ANNE LAMBELET

FERIA DE SEVILLA

PAGE STREET KIDS

Maria loved a lot of things.

She loved tea parties and dancing
and wearing her hair in pigtails,
but more than anything
in the world . . .

Maria loved **CHURROS**.

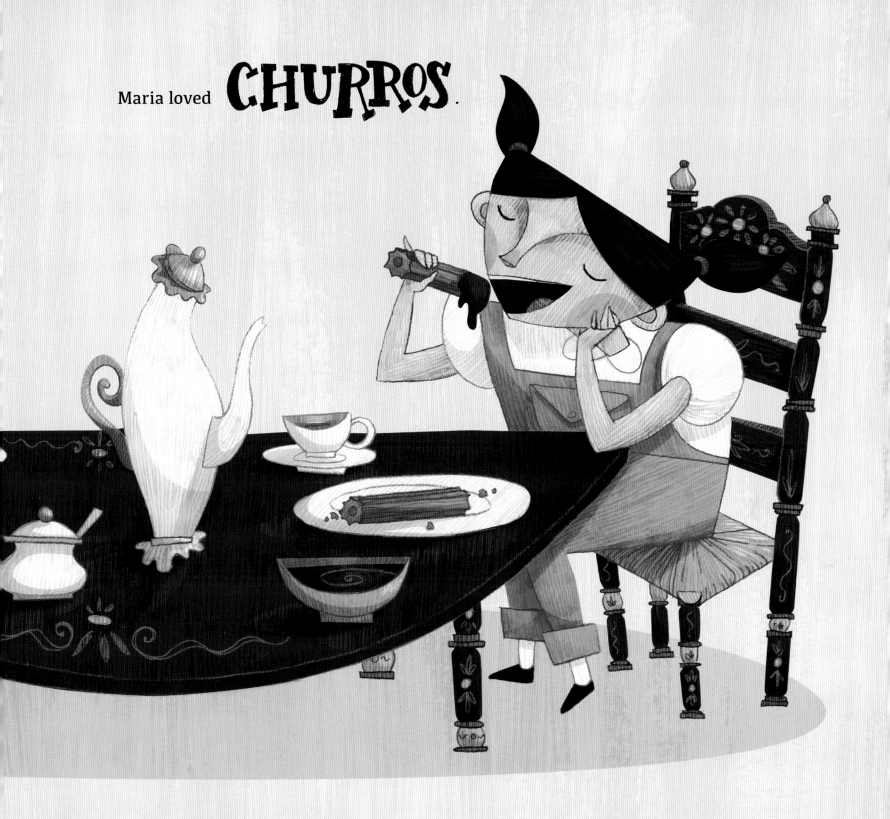

She couldn't see a churro
without needing a taste,

she couldn't taste a churro
without having to finish it,

and she could never finish one churro without wanting

MORE CHURROS!

So when she saw a poster advertising a bullfight, she knew that the grand prize had to be hers. She'd never be left wanting more churros again!

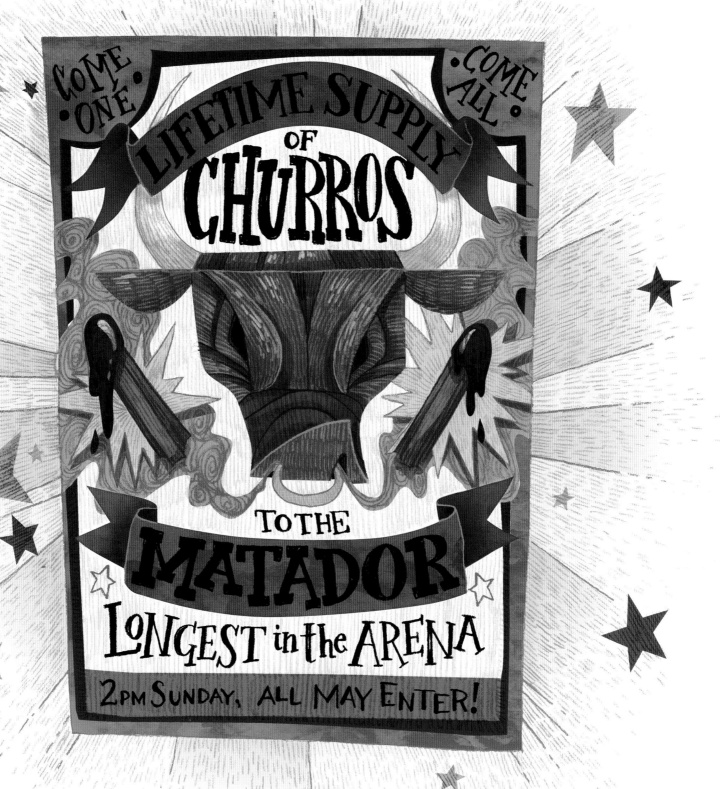

But *Maria* was one of the smallest little girls in all of Spain.

She wasn't **FAST** enough to outrun the bull.

She wasn't **STRONG** enough to intimidate the bull.

She wasn't **BIG** enough to overpower the bull.

If she couldn't fight the bull, then how could she possibly win a bullfight?

If only there was someone she could turn to for advice . . .

When **Maria** joined the other matadors on the big day, none of them could believe their eyes.

HA HA HA HA

"You cannot possibly be *FAST* enough to fight the bull!" said the fastest matador.

"You cannot possibly be **STRONG** enough!" said the strongest.

"You cannot possibly be **BIG** enough!" said the biggest.

"You should just give up now," they all agreed.
"There is no way such a little girl could ever fight such an enormous bull."

Maria tried her best to ignore them and
to think only of the promise of her beloved churros,

but the more they all laughed at her,
the more worried she became.

Then the bullfight began,
and one by one,
each of the matadors took their turn.

The bull was *FASTER* than the fastest matador,
STRONGER than the strongest matador,
and even **BIGGER** than the biggest matador.

One by one,
they faced the bull
and one by one,
they were defeated . . .

Finally, *Maria* entered the ring.
In the center of the arena waited the most
ferocious-looking bull she had ever seen,

but she marched up to him anyway,

picturing churros for courage . . .

and asked the bull to *dance*.

After years of being battered and bullied
by every matador he'd ever met,
the bull's heart was so warmed
by the little girl's request
that he couldn't
help but say,
"Yes!"

As they took their bows,
the crowd burst into thunderous applause.

And **Maria** and her new friend gratefully accepted their prize.